A
CELEBRATION
BOOK

given by

****

Carolyn Webber

In honor of
The 1995-96 kindergarten

Pig Pig and the Magic Photo Album

by David McPhail

E. P. DUTTON · NEW YORK

for Patrick
Hello, Paddy Boy

Library of Congress Cataloging in Publication Data
McPhail, David M.
   Pig Pig and the magic photo album.
   Summary: While waiting to have his picture taken,
Pig Pig practices saying "Cheese" as he looks through
a photo album and is amazed at the outcome.
   [1. Pigs—Fiction.   2. Humorous stories] I. Title.
PZ7.M2427Pg   1986   [E]   85-20459
ISBN 0-525-44238-3

Published in the United States by E. P. Dutton,
2 Park Avenue, New York, N.Y. 10016,
a subsidiary of NAL Penguin Inc.
Published simultaneously in Canada by
Fitzhenry & Whiteside Limited, Toronto
Editor: Ann Durell   Designer: Riki Levinson
Printed in Hong Kong by South China Printing Co.
First Edition   COBE   10 9 8 7 6 5 4 3 2

Pig Pig was all dressed up,
waiting to have his picture taken.

While he waited, Pig Pig practiced saying
"Cheese." And while he practiced, he looked
at a photo album that the photographer had
brought along.

He looked a long time at a picture of a church
with a tall steeple.
"Cheese," said Pig Pig to himself.
And WHAM . . .

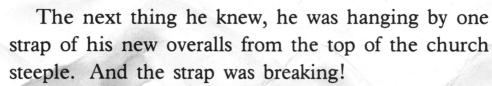

The next thing he knew, he was hanging by one strap of his new overalls from the top of the church steeple. And the strap was breaking!

Quickly, Pig Pig turned to a picture of a pilot in a small open plane.

"Cheese!" he shouted.

And in a flash, he was sitting on the wing
of the airplane, flying through the clouds.
But he was sliding off the plane.
Pig Pig turned to a picture of a rowboat.
"Cheese!" he cried.

And there he was, sitting in the rowboat.
Unfortunately, he was also sitting on someone's guitar.
But before the person could do anything about it, the
boat drifted under a tree, and Pig Pig climbed quickly
onto a branch.

He breathed a sigh of relief. He was safe . . . except for the big hungry-looking crocodile that was swimming toward him with its mouth open.

The branch started to crack.
Pig Pig looked at a picture of
a birthday party.
"Cheese!" he said.

And there he was, at the party.
"Chocolate!" squealed Pig Pig. "My favorite!"
"Get that pig out of my cake!" a little boy screamed.

A man tried to grab Pig Pig, but he dashed along

the tabletop and out the door into the garden.

On the far side of the garden was a big iron gate, and as Pig Pig ran toward it, he heard fierce barking and howling behind him.

Dogs were after him!

Pig Pig ran faster than he had ever run before. But the dogs ran even faster. They were gaining on him!

Pig Pig threw himself at the gate. It was locked.
With the dogs closing in, he opened the photo
album . . . to a picture of his very own living room.
"Cheese!" shouted Pig Pig.

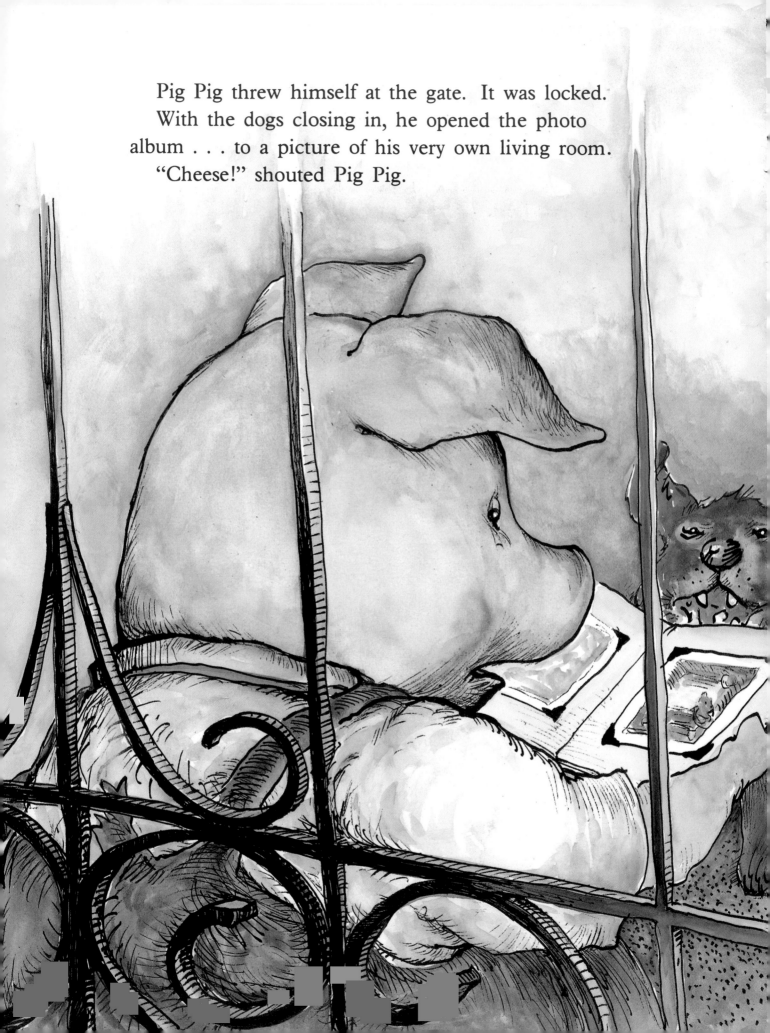

He was HOME!

"Pig Pig, you're a fright!" cried his mother.

"Go change your clothes and wash your face."

When Pig Pig returned, he sat very still and looked right into the camera. He smiled his biggest smile . . . but he absolutely refused to say "CHEESE."